Gosha Ramchandra

Jesus in the Vedas

The testimony of Hindu scriptures in corroboration of the rudiments of

Christian doctrine

Gosha Ramchandra

Jesus in the Vedas
The testimony of Hindu scriptures in corroboration of the rudiments of Christian doctrine

ISBN/EAN: 9783337391843

Printed in Europe, USA, Canada, Australia, Japan

Cover: Foto ©Andreas Hilbeck / pixelio.de

More available books at **www.hansebooks.com**

JESUS IN THE VEDAS;

OR,

The Testimony of Hindu Scriptures in Corroboration of the Rudiments

OF

CHRISTIAN DOCTRINE

BY

A NATIVE INDIAN MISSIONARY

~~~~~~~~

FUNK & WAGNALLS COMPANY

NEW YORK

LONDON   TORONTO

1892

Printed in the United States

JESUS IN THE VEDAS.

THE Christian scheme of salvation is thus epitomized by St. Paul: "Now, therefore, ye are no more strangers and foreigners, but fellow-citizens with the saints, and of the household of God ; and are built upon the foundation of the Apostles and Prophets, Jesus Christ himself being the chief corner-stone."[1] This household is a "kingdom," and it is a "kingdom prepared from the foundation of the world."[2] It has also a roll or register in which all its members are noted down, the roll being otherwise called "the book of life of the Lamb slain from the founda-

---
[1] Eph. ii. 19, 20. [2] Matt. xxv. 34.

tion of the world."[1] And this discloses that inscrutable ruling of our Creator and Supreme Governor that "without shedding of blood is no remission."[2]

This rule or law is above human logic. Into the policy of Heavenly jurisprudence, it would be a presumption to pry. The finite can never grasp the infinite, or examine it like a *berry in the hand*. Once satisfied that it is God's will and God's decree, and that it meets a human difficulty and solves a spiritual problem, man's duty is to accept the solution.

To inquire into the *fact* of His decree and His declaration is only the exercise of a prerogative which has been vested in the human mind by the Author of our being. It is both a privilege and a duty to examine the evidence of the fact, but the fact being found, and the decree being authenticated, that "the Lord has laid on him

---

[1] Rev. xiii. 8. [2] Heb. ix. 22.

the iniquity of us all," and that "with his stripes we are healed," we must remember that a decree is intended for obedience and guidance, not for wrangling and disputation.

Such is the Christian scheme. It has for its corner-stone the Sacrifice of the Lamb slain from the foundation of the world. It involves the inscrutable law of Infinite Wisdom and Heavenly Counsel that without shedding of blood there is no remission. It was available for human salvation from the moment that it had become necessary for it. The principles of Adam's religion, in the primitive age, were thus the same as ours, now in the fulness of time. Reference was made to it on the Fall of our first parents, and the introduction of sin. The seed of the woman[1] was no other than the Lamb slain from the foundation of the world. His sacrifice, though accomplished in him, was commemorated

---

[1] Gen. iii. 15.

and typified from the beginning. The primeval
institution of Sacrifices is evident from the practice of Abel, who "by faith offered a more
excellent sacrifice than Cain, by which he
obtained witness that he was righteous, God
testifying of his gifts, and by it, he, being dead,
yet speaketh."[1] The same was again typified in
the offerings which Noah presented on the altar
he had builded, and they met with the same
result of God's acceptance, for we are told, "the
Lord smelt a sweet savor."[2] The identical
practice under a similar persuasion we notice in
the time of Job, who offered burnt offerings
"continually," saying, "It may be that my sons
have sinned and cursed God in their hearts."[3]
These are indisputable facts. They manifest
the way in which pious souls betook themselves
to "the Lamb of God which taketh away the sin
of the world."[4] They indicate the hopes which

---

[1] Heb. xi. 4. [2] Gen. viii. 21. [3] Job i. 5. [4] John i. 29.

inspired those "that looked for redemption in Israel."[1]

We may fairly presume from these recorded instances of Abel's, Noah's, and Job's offerings that they were consequent on the institution of such sacrifices from the beginning under divine direction, at once commemorative, and prefigurative, of the great sacrifice of "the Lamb slain from the foundation of the world." Noah was not many generations distant from Adam, and he could have introduced and kept up in the post-diluvian world what he knew to have been ordained before the Deluge. Speaking now from the Christian point of view, we can reasonably conclude that the sacrifices, acceptably offered by the patriarchs we have named, were typical of the great sacrifice accomplished on Mount Calvary which they foreshadowed. For "other foundation can no man lay than that is laid,

---

[1] Luke ii. 38.

which is Jesus Christ." [1] Nor is it possible "that
the blood of bulls and of goats should take away
sins," [2] in any age or country. It was, to use
and adapt a Vedic expression, only a *foreshad-
owing of the truly Saving Sacrifice.* [3]

Assuming, then, that the offering of sacrifices
was a recognized institution from the early days
of Noah in the post-diluvian world, it might be
reasonably expected that the practice would not
immediately die away. If Noah and Job knew
what they were about, and performed the offerings with the solemnity of religious ceremonies,
each would instruct his own children and grand-
children in what he would necessarily consider
as the first and most important duty of the
human race. The practice would thus be transmitted to their posterity as a binding Divine institution. The institution would, doubtless, be

---

[1] 1. Cor. iii. 11.   [2] Heb. x. 4.   [3] "Tândya-mâha Brâhmana,"
vol. i. p. 332.

maintained with the tenacity with which men usually keep up practices derived from their immediate superiors and forefathers, and never allow any to fall into desuetude without valid reasons. They would, indeed, be cherished as heirlooms out of respect for their parents, and nothing short of a mental or social revolution could account for their entire extinction. Such a revolution, again, might be expected to be a fact as notorious as that which originally caused the initiation of the practice which it overturned.

The institution we are speaking of would *as a fact* be therefore capable of proof or disproof from the history of Noah's descendants, by which we mean the history of mankind. The perpetuation of the practice would be corroborative of the institution and of the principles which originated it, while its entire neglect, without a valid cause, would tend to damage the presumption of its divine origin. If the practice were found in vogue among mankind for countless generations, and never fallen into oblivion without such a counter movement as we have suggested, the fact would add no small weight to the reasons for which we have presumed its divine original. If, on the contrary, the practice were wholly lost sight of after the days of Noah, such an abrupt discontinuance must weaken those reasons.

We must here add that it is only the overt acts, the offerings and ceremonies which, if true, we would expect to find in the history of mankind. The theology, or the doctrine involved, might be insensibly perverted, or even die away altogether, through ignorance or mental imbecility. Tradition may keep up a practice or festival involving overt acts, but it is not adequate for the perpetuation of the doctrine or idea which originated the practice. The perpetuation of a ceremony by imitating one's father's practice, patent to the eye, is easier than the psychological process of rightly comprehending and correctly teaching the dogma or sentiment which initiated the ceremony.

But while ignorance or misconception of the doctrine or event involved in, or supposed to be commemorated by, a practice, perpetuated as a visible ceremony, detracts nothing from the corroborative evidence we have mentioned before, and is therefore no disproof of that doctrine, its actual transmission, along with the practice, even in a distorted form, adds considerable strength to that evidence. The institution of sacrifices was, as we have already asserted, typical of Him who "was once offered to bear the sins of many."[1] The continued prevalence of the practice among the families of men would itself be corroborative evidence of the original institution, and there could be no detraction from

---

[1] Heb. ix. 28.

it, even if it appeared anywhere that it was maintained in ignorance of the doctrine it was intended to commemorate. For people might have
perpetuated the visible ceremony without comprehending its psychological cause. But if we
find in any place that, along with the perpetuation of the practice, there was a traditional
teaching that the ceremony had the mysterious
power of abolishing sin and depriving death of
its terrors, the fact would add still greater force
to our argument.

Men have not been wanting to assail, as far as
they could, the integrity of God's truth, and
especially that portion of it, which is indeed its
chief corner-stone, the Sacrifice *of the Lamb of
God which taketh away the sin of the world.*
Their weapons of aggression have only been in
theories, imperfect in their parts, and too often
with hasty generalizations, but those settled results in which the body of philosophers agree,

far from contradicting Scripture, "often confirm and illustrate the statements of the Inspired Volume." [1] The direct evidences on which all teaching of God's revelation rests, are in themselves quite sufficient for giving an intelligent "reason for the faith" that is in us, as against high-sounding cavils. The palpable and unmistakable tendency of infidelity to overturn the moral basis on which society is founded, and by virtue whereof it maintains its sacred institutions for the public weal, is also sufficient in itself to serve as a lesson and warning, which can only endear the doctrine of the Cross to all lovers of purity and order, and impel them to cling to their "rock" of defense with greater tenacity than ever before.

We have given above a brief summary of the Scriptural account of the institution of Sacrifices and the doctrine therein involved. We need not

[1] Pratt's "Scripture and Science Not at Variance," p. 371.

repeat that the cardinal teaching of Christianity is connected therewith; our business now is to show the extent to which the Hindu records testify to the *fact* of the institution and approximate to the doctrine typified by it.

The practice of sacrifices, as a mode of propitiating the gods or supernatural powers, has indeed existed among all nations. We do not, however, know of any nation which manifested such an intelligible view of the underlying doctrines as the primitive Hindus did in their early writings. Nor have we seen, outside the limits of Jewry wherein "God was known," such an approximation to the Scriptural teaching on the subject as is found in ancient Hindu records.

The most prominent feature of the Vedic religion is its sacrifices. Scarcely a hymn is found in which sacrifice is not alluded to. The very first verse of the very first hymn runs: "I glorify Agni, the high priest (*purshit*) of the sacri-

fice, the divine ministrant who presents the obla-
tion (to the gods), and is the possessor of great
wealth." The expression translated by Prof.
Wilson, "high-priest of the Sacrifice," rendered
by Dr. Baneryea, *the foremost minister of the
Sacrifice.* Here Agni is so called. In the first
of the hymns to the Maruts, with which Max
Müller commences his translation of the Rig-veda
we find a similar reference. The eighth verse
reads: "With the beloved hosts of Indra, with
the blameless heaven-tending (Maruts), the sacrificer cries aloud." The separate history of the
Aryan family whether Hindu, Iranian, Teutonic,
or Keltic can go no further back than these
hymns. In them sacrifices are spoken of as if
they were coeval with man. They occupy the
foremost place in importance, and apparently in
age, in the Indo-Aryan worship.

There are numerous passages in this most ancient of hymn-books, most conclusively proving

(?)

that the ancient Hindus regarded sacrifice as the most sacred act in their worship. It and its symbol of success, fire, were regarded as the "navel of the world." [1] The two most prominent deities in the hymns are Agni and Indra. And the importance of both is most intimately associated with the sacrifice. The first as we have seen is its chief ministrant, the second its most regular attendant. The sacrifice undoubtedly existed before there were priests set apart for its celebration, when the householder was high-priest in his own family.

Although we have analytically arrived at our conclusions after due investigation of certain premises, we shall not follow that system on the present occasion; but shall *first* declare the results and then submit the proofs. Accordingly we now enunciate two propositions to be made good on documentary evidence.

---

[1] "Rig-veda," i. 59, 12; 104, 35.

The two propositions are :

First. That the fundamental principles of Christian doctrine in relation to the salvation of the world find a remarkable counterpart in the Vedic principles of primitive Hinduism in relation to the destruction of sin, and the redemption of the sinner by the efficacy of Sacrifice, itself a figure of *Prajâpati*, the Lord and Saviour of the Creation, who had given himself up as an offering for that purpose.

Second. That the meaning of *Prajâpati*, an appellation, variously described as a *Purusha* begotten in the beginning, as Visvakarman, the Creator of all, singularly coincides with the meaning of the name and offices of the historical reality JESUS CHRIST, and that no other person than JESUS of Nazareth has ever appeared in the world claiming the character and position of the self-sacrificing *Prajâpati*, at the same time both mortal and immortal.

As to the definition of the terms which constitute our main question in these propositions, Christianity itself is known tolerably well to all educated persons. Notwithstanding a variety of denominations, it is generally understood and acknowledged that every one who calls himself a Christian considers it to be a scheme of reconciliation of man with God through the meritorious sacrifice of CHRIST, "the Lamb of God who taketh away the sin of the world," who is Himself both God and man. The definition of Hinduism is not so obvious. On one point, however, all Hindus are agreed. They all refer to the Vedas as the sacred oracles of their religion. We must, therefore, for the purposes of this discourse, define Hinduism as the religion of the Vedas—the more so, since its records inevitably lead us to the conclusion that both caste and idolatry are later accretions in the simpler systems taught in the Vedas.

And as to the idolatrous worship of the popular gods which now prevails, there is not even an inkling of it to be found in the primitive Vedas. And the Veda, where it does in one place refer to the four orders, speaks of them as the creatures of circumstances. The *Brahmans* were no other than priests necessary for the celebration of sacrificial rites, and the *Vaisyas*, the third order, were the laity of Hinduism, the term itself having the same signification. Whereas the second and fourth orders are expressly declared to have been created afterward for the defence and menial service of the Commonwealth respectively.

To do justice to Hinduism, therefore, we must look at its original form as disclosed in the Vedas both in doctrine and in ritual; the doctrine as laid down dogmatically, and the ritual as perpetuated practically in illustration of the doctrine. In this respect it must be admitted that inconsistencies will often be discovered; we shall meet with conflicting doctrines and self-contradictory precepts. But we shall endeavor to present as fair a view as truth and justice can allow. We shall eschew pessimism and avoid undue optimism.

In all communities Theology commences with cosmogony. It is in the dependence of the creature upon his Creator that the religious sentiment in human nature is founded. There can be no loyalty without a recognized ruling power, nor can there be any religion in the absence of an acknowledged supernatural Power as Creator of the world. And it is from the *seen* that ideas of the *unseen* are derived. What the Indian *Nyâya* says is most true : the *anumnâa* or inference must have some *pratyaksha* or perception for its basis. And this refers to things intellectual as well as things physical. External observation and internal sensation may each justify an inference or conclusion. The visible universe leads to the conviction of an invisible Cause of all things. The complicated and curiously subtle adaptations we notice all around, their aptitude for certain ends, to which they are directly tending, force the conviction on the mind that there must be a Creator who made all these things and adapted them to their specific ends. This is the commencement of Theology. The human mind at once detects in the visible world, and its adaptation of means to ends, the finger of an invisible but all intelligent and beneficent Creator, whom it invests with infinite goodness, power, and wisdom, that is to say, with all the goodness, power, and wisdom which the mind itself can conceive. How and with what materials the Deity has created the world is a question which the mind in its native simplicity, untainted by the subtleties of a corrupt philosophy, does not stop to inquire. It may, in a rude and uncultivated state, mistake something, itself a creature, astoundingly striking to the eye or the ear, such as the sun or moon, thunder or lightning, to be the creator of the world, but it never thinks of launching into difficulties on the subject of the *material* cause, unless entangled in the mazes of skepticism, in speculations which are beyond its own depth, and are only the suggestions of human vanity and conceit. We find accordingly that in the earliest period of our history, as disclosed in the Rig-veda, our primitive ancestors had clear and decided conceptions of Deity, independent of philosophic speculations, and untainted with the subtle casuistry of a later age. They did not, indeed, understand the true nature of creation—the calling anything into being out of nothing—but neither, on the other hand, did they deny the possibility of such creation. That question did not arise in their minds, they did not discuss it. But they confidently declared that the heavens and earth were established by their celestial *Varuna*,[1] whom, after their neighbors, the Iranians, they styled *Asura-pracheta* and *Asura-visvaveda*, which was the Sanskrit translation of the Zendic Ahura-Mazda. It is, however, difficult to say that the Vedic dogma was pure monotheism, untainted by polytheism. At the same time I must confess that those, who delight in charging those most ancient records with the gross corruptions of a later period, forget three important points clearly inculcated in the Veda. These three points are the following:

Firstly.—The Rig-veda declares in several places[2] the existence of one unborn or eternal being as different from and superior to *Devas* and *Asuras*, and far above heaven and earth.

Secondly.—The same Veda declares that the

---

[1] "Rig-veda," i. 24, 7, 8 ; viii. 42, 1.   [2] i. 164, 6; ii. 27, 10; x. 82.

Devas were originally and by birth mortals like men, and that they got to heaven by virtue of the Sacrifice.

Thirdly.—The Rig-veda, again, as if to apologize for an incipient polytheism that was growing up, declares dogmatically that all the gods, though differently named aud represented, are in reality one—πολλῶν ὀνομάτων μορφὴ μία: "They call him Indra, Mitra, Varuna, Agni ; and (he is) the celestial, well-winged Garutmat. Sages name variously that which is but one : they call it Agni, Yama, Mâtarisvan." [1]

It is not necessary for the purposes of this discourse to dilate on this point. Some texts of the Vedas at least have acknowledged the existence of one Supreme Essence who is above all. There are other texts where speculations with an atheistic tendency may be discovered ; but such speculations are everywhere found to be indulged

---

[1] "Rig-veda," i. 164, 46.

in by a few forward and generally conceited intellects. We shall pass them over here and proceed to consider the religious practices, the rites and ceremonies, by means of which our primitive ancestors gave practical effect to their theology, and to that sentiment of devotion which had distinguished the Indo-Aryans from the beginning.

Now the first and foremost rites of religion which they regularly celebrated, and on which they most firmly relied as the great cure for all the evils of life, and the secret of all success in the world, were *sacrificial* rites. Not idolatrous worship, not observances of caste, but *yajna* (sacrifice), and its connectives were the religious rites cherished by them.

The rites of Sacrifice were called "the first and primary rites," and this was because the first man after the deluge, whom the Hindus called *Manu*, and the Hebrews *Noah* or *Nuh*, had offered a burnt-offering, which was held by all his successors as the first and most important ceremony of religion. The high estimation in which the rite of Sacrifice is held in the Vedas will appear (1) from the date and authorship assigned for its institution, (2) the great virtues attributed to its performance, both for spiritual and temporal purposes, (3) the benefit it is said to have conferred on the gods themselves. We shall briefly review it under these different aspects.

First. The authorship of the institution is attributed to "Creation's Lord" himself, and its date is reckoned as coeval with the creation. "Creation's Lord instituted the sacrifice. He uttered the *Nivid* (sacrificial formula), all things were created after it." [1] In the post-diluvian world, the first act of the surviving patriarch, whom the Indo-Aryans called *Manu* (a

---

[1] "Aitareya-brâhmana," vol. i., p. 48.

name not very dissimilar to the Semitic *Nu*),
was a sacrificial offering. This latter tradition
is confirmed as well by the Bible as also by the
account found in the Assyrian Inscriptions. It
will not be regarded as an extreme act of credu-
lity if we declare that much consideration is due
to the concurrence of so many curious traditions.
With reference to the legend of the institution
of sacrifice being coeval with the creation, we
can only interpret the writer's meaning in the
sense of that institution having existed from
time *immemorial*. The Vedas knew of no time
when it was not practiced.

Second. With reference to the great virtues
attributed to the celebration of Sacrifices, it was
considered as the potent remedy for all evils—
the panacea for all distempers. Even the briny
ocean and the dust of the earth distill sweets for
the regular performer of the sacrificial ritual.[1]

---

[1] " Rig-veda," i. 90, 6.

The world was called into being by virtue of Sacrifice and is still upheld by its force, being indeed its "navel." [1]

In it lay all strength against enemies. The Zand-Avasta, too, concurred with the Vedas here. The evil spirit had asked *Zarathustra:* "By whose word wilt thou smite, by whose word wilt thou annihilate, by what well-made arms smite my creatures?" *Zarathustra* answered boldly: "Mortar, cup, Haoma, and the word which *Ahuza-Mazda* has spoken—these are my best weapons." [2] And these were the implements of Sacrifice.

Nor was the virtue of Sacrifice less conspicuous from a spiritual point of view. It was the great means of escape from the pernicious effects of sin. "Give us, O Indra, multitudes of good

---

[1] "Rig-veda," i. 59, 12 ; i. 164, 35.   [2] "Bleeck," i., p. 44.

horses with which we may offer our oblations.
and thereby escape all sins."[1]

"Do thou lead us safe through all sins by the
way of Sacrifice."[2]

"Do thou (O Sacrificial Soma), who knowest
all things, make us to pass over sin, as a navi-
gator ferries men over the sea."

Varuna, whose name appears the same as the
Greek word for heaven (Οὐρανός) and who, as we
have seen, was regarded as the Supreme Being
under the title of *Asura-prachetas*, is then in-
voked for such knowledge as may make us wise
unto salvation. "O illustrious Varuna, do thou
quicken our understanding—we that are practicing this ceremony, that we may embark on the
good ferrying boat by which we may escape all
sins."[3] On this passage the Aitarya-brâhmana
remarks: "Sacrifice is the good ferrying boat.

---

[1] "Rig veda," x. 113, 10. [2] "Rig-veda," x. 311, 6. [3] "Rig-
veda," viii. 42, 3.

The black skin is the good ferrying boat. The Word is the good ferrying boat. Having embarked on the Word, one crosses over to the heavenly world." [1]

It was not unusual in those days for ferryboats to be made of leather ; reminding us not only of Noah's ark, but also of the words in the Baptismal Service of the Church of England— that he "may be received into the ark of Christ's Church, and may so pass the waves of this troublesome world, that he may finally come to the land of everlasting life." The "black skin" and the "Word" above mentioned are explained in the Sátapatha-bráhmana, where "Sacrifice" is represented as retreating from the gods in a *black* form. They found it and took off its skin, and thence was produced the three-fold knowl edge (Veda) which, as a product of the Sacrifice, is identified with "the good ferrying boat."

----

[1] p. 10.

"Sacrifice was retreating from the gods. It was going about in a black form. The gods having found it, tore off its skin and took it. The same is the three-fold knowledge, Sacrifice." [1] This accounts for the "boat" being assimilated with "the black skin" and "the Word"—the latter two being inseparable from the "Sacrifice," which is also here declared, "the three-fold knowledge," otherwise called the Veda or its "Word." Another reason for assimilating the saving boat with the "Word" is, that there was actually a hymn which was called *plava*, "raft" or "boat," and it was to be used daily.

Sacrifice offered according to the true way—the right path—has been held in the Rik, Yajush, and Sâman to be the good ferrying boat or raft by which he may escape from sin. It was expressly declared to be the authorized

---

[1] "Sâtapathâ-brâhmana," p. 8.

(3)

means both for remission and annulment of sin.
"The animal he offers to Agnisoma is his own
ransom." [1]

That Sacrifice was held as the great means for
procuring remission or annulment of sins of
every description, is declared in numerous passages—not only by the figures of saving boats or
rafts, but literally in express terms. The following formula gives the words which were uttered
by the sacrificer as he offered each limb to the
Fire in slaughtering and cutting up the victims:
"O thou (animal limb, now being consigned to
the fire), thou art the annulment of sins committed by gods. Thou art the annulment of
sins committed by the (departed) fathers. Thou
art the annulment of sins committed by men.
Thou art the annulment of sins committed by
ourselves. Whatever sins we have committed
by day or by night, thou art the annulment

[1] "Taittiriya-samhitâ," vol. i., p. 369.

thereof. Whatever sins we have committed sleeping or waking thou art the annulment thereof. Whatever sins we have committed, knowing or unknowing, thou art the annulment thereof. Thou art the annulment of sin—of sin." [1] In this extraordinary passage it will be observed that the Sacrifice was regarded in one word, and that a Biblical one—as "a propitiation for the sins of the whole world." And though "it is not possible that the blood of bulls and of goats should take away sin," it may be the type or shadow of the blood of the "Lamb slain from the foundation of the world," which was appointed by God for this express purpose. When we consider such texts we may well conclude, even independently of Revelation, that from the beginning men regarded Sacrifice as an act of worship of the highest importance.

The Vedic sacrifices were doubtless curious and

---

[1] "Tândya-mahâbrâhmana," vol. i., p. 55.

peculiar in themselves. They were not intended merely for the gratification of particular gods or supernatural powers having a relish for the fumes of fat burnt offerings. They seem to have had a higher object in view. The limb of the victim as it was thrown into the Fire was ac- costed *as the annulment of sin*—not only the sacrificer's own sins, but the sins of all gods and men—that is to say, of the whole world. And along with this, we have the self-sacrifice of *Prajâpati*, the Lord of Creatures, the *Purusha*, begotten in the beginning of the world, out of whose limbs, as the body was cut up, sprang the different orders of men of which Indian society was composed.

Legends such as these naturally suggest the question of the origin of such conceptions in the Aryan mind. Doubtless, we recognize in them a hazy representation or distorted view of the great mystery of Christianity, *the Lamb slain from the foundation of the world*, and of the church, which was *his body*, the household of God, the spiritual society comprehending all believers. But how came the Aryans to have got any insight into such a mystery so early as the age of the Vedas?

Abel's and Noah's sacrifices were accepted—the former having been so by reason of *the sacrificer's faith;* and of the latter, it is recorded that *the Lord smelt a sweet savor.* The last words are parallel to the concluding expressions in Eph. v. 2: " As Christ also hath loved us, and hath given himself for us, an offering and a sacrifice to God for A SWEET SMELLING SAVOR. It is inconceivable that Abel's and Noah's sacrifices should be described as we find them to be, unless they were typical of the great Sacrifice mentioned in the text just cited, and unless both sacrificers were cognizant, to some extent at least, of the mystery of *the Lamb slain*

from the foundation of the world. And there
is no reason to suppose that either of them would
put his candle under a bushel. Whatever they
may have learnt by divine revelation on the subject would he naturally communicated to their
children and contemporaries, and thus the teaching might somehow be transmitted to the Indo-
Aryan family—subject of course to such errors
and distortions as were unavoidable under the
circumstances. The stream of Truth is always
liable to be tainted and colored as it flows over
the soil of human tradition.

Our ancestors seem to have understood, or at
least suspected, that "it is not possible that the
blood of bulls and of goats should take away
sins." Our ancestors could not be entirely un-
conscious of that. And notwithstanding their
hazy conceptions of *scape-goat*, and of the self-
sacrifice of the Lord of Creatures, they felt a
difficulty. The sacrificial ritual was more easily

perpetuated than its meaning or purport understood, or communicated. It was difficult for
recollections of the unwritten theology, on
which it may have been originally founded, to
be preserved in their purity from generation to
generation. The conception of the principles
which underlay the institution of the ceremony
had been, perhaps, well-nigh forgotten. The
ritual was held as an *opus operatum*. There
would be little difficulty for children to keep it
up exactly as they saw their fathers perform it.
The underlying doctrine in the absence of writ-
ten records could not be so easily transmitted by
tradition. The correct learning and correct
transmission of *doctrine* always requires closer
attention, and greater intellectual effort on the
part both of preceptor and pupil, than the mi-
nute observation and imitation of external ceremonies. The ritual itself may have had "a
shadow of good things to come, but could not

with those sacrifices offered year by year make the comers thereunto perfect."

To what extent the Indo-Aryans had correctly comprehended the doctrine on which sacrificial ceremonies were founded, we cannot easily guess. But we find they considered it a mystery or *mâyâ*. Thus: "O death! the thousand myriads of thy hands for the destruction of mortals, we annul them all by the *mâyâ* or mysterious power of sacrifice."[1] The doctrine involved, whether the Indo-Aryans rightly understood it or not, is doubtless a "mystery." Many things connected with the inscrutable will of the Almighty *must* be mysterious.

Third. They had the same conception of this mysterious power in the case of the Divas who were "originally mortals," who were "in the beginning like men," but had been "translated to heaven by the virtue of sacrifice." Indra himself

[1] "Taittiriya-âranyaka," p. 198.

was no better at first. He was "our man," and, as such, the "best of men." But, like other gods, though more excellently than any other, he had performed numberless sacrifices, and been thereby promoted to heaven, free from "want, misery, and death." Again, "by this sacrificial hymn the gods had overcome the *Asuras*. By the same does the sacrificer, whoever he be, still overcome the most wicked enemy (sin)." [1]

And it has been expressly declared that as sacrifice was the way by which the *Divas* got to heaven, the same is still the way open for mankind. "Whosoever desires the felicity of heaven, let him perform sacrifices in the right way." And such performances were reckoned as the first acts of religion, the first and primitive *dhanna*. The *Divas* performed a sacrifice by means of a sacrifice. These were the first acts of religion. They became glorified and

---

[1] "Tândya-Mahâbrâhmana," vol. i. p. 105.

attained to heaven, where the pristine Sâdhyas
live.[1]

Now the secret of this extreme importance
attached to sacrifice, and the key to the proper
understanding of the whole subject was the self-
sacrifice[2] of *Prajâpati*, the Lord or Supporter of
the Creation, the "*Purusha* begotten before the
world," "the *Visvakarman*, the Author of the
Universe." The idea is found in all the three
Vedas—Rik, Yajusha, and Sâman—in Samhitâs,
Brâhmanas. Arânyakas, and Upanishads. The
Divine *Purusha* who gave himself up as a sacrifice for the *Divas, i. e. emancipated mortals*,
had, it is said, desired and got a mortal body
fit for sacrifice, and himself became *half mortal* and *half immortal*. It is added that he
made sacrifice a reflection or figure of himself;
that the *equine* body was found fit for sacrifice,

---

[1] "Rig-veda," i. 164, 50. [2] "Tândya-mahâbrâhmana," vol. i.
p. 410.

and that whenever a horse-sacrifice was solem-
nized, it became no other than an offering of *himself*. This idea of the "Lord of Creatures"
offering himself a sacrifice for the benefit of the
Divas, who were then but mortals, is also found,
but in a more complicated form, in the celebrated
Purushasûkta. It would not be easy to account
for the genesis of such an idea except on the
assumption of some primitive tradition of the
"Lamb slain from the foundation of the world,"
who was "over all, God blessed forever."

The idea of the sacrifice of a Divine Person is
not found merely in a single isolated passage, in
which case it might have been explained away;
but in various passages in the different Vedas it
finds expression in different ways, sometimes
clearly, sometimes obscurely; and, taken as a
whole, it appears a prominent doctrine, which
gives signification to the frequent exhortations
to the performance of sacrificial rites and cere-

monies. The same idea throws light on the texts which declare the celebration of Sacrifice to be the only way of attaining heaven, after the example of those quondam mortals, the *Divas*; and the only good vessel for getting over the waves of sin, which would otherwise overwhelm mankind. Both the Rik and the Yajush tell us that "When the gods, celebrating the sacrifice, bound *Purusha* as the victim, they immolated Him, the Sacrifice, on the grass—even him, the *Purusha*, who was begotten in the beginning."[1]

There is again an obscure passage in the "Rig-veda," which Yâska, the author of the "Nirukta," thus expounds: "Visva-Karman had in universal sacrifice offered all creatures, and then eventually offered Himself also."

The Yajush summarizes the same passage by putting into the mouth of the Divine Self-Sacri-

---

[1] "Taittiriya-âranyaka," pp. 331–333.

ficer the words: "Let me offer myself in all creatures, and all creatures in myself." [1]

The obscurity is not removed by these different readings. The idea is nevertheless somewhat cleared up by the light of other passages, and by the assistance of the Bible. The world was condemned, and offered for sacrifice, that is to say, was devoted to destruction, for sin; and the Divine Saviour then offered Himself for its deliverance. The Bible says, "If one died for all, then were all dead." The Veda says, conversely, *Because all were devoted to destruction, therefore one died for all.* The one reasoned from the consequent to the antecedent; the other from the antecedent to the consequent; but both appeared to concur in the nature of the antecedent and the consequent.

The Brihadâranyaka, itself an upanishad, says, "*Prajâpati* desired to offer a great Sacrifice.

---

[1] "Sátapatha-bráhmana," 13, 7, 1.

He desired :—May I have a body proper for sacrifice, and may I become embodied by it."

The same upanishad adds ; "Priests solemnize the sacrifice as if it were an offering of *Prajâ-pati* himself, or the universal Godhead." Again, "it (the sacrifice) becomes an only Divata, even Death," which, to borrow for the moment a Biblical phrase, *reigns over all.* And then the same sacrifice eventually "conquers death, nor can death get to it again."

The Satapatha-brâhmana says with reference to *Prajâpati* that "half of himself was mortal and half immortal." [1] Again, "when he had given himself up for them, he made a figure or image of himself, which is sacrifice. Therefore they say, *Prajâpati* is the sacrifice Himself."

Prajâpati or *Purusha* is elsewhere spoken of as *Atmadâ* or "giver of self," whose "shadow,

---

[1] x. 1, 3, 1. Müller's "Hibbert Lectures," p. 297.

whose death, is immortality" (to us).[1] And this immortality, again, regarded not only the soul but the body also. Thus in the "Rig-veda" the son of a righteous man was instructed to use the following formula in his last address to his dead father: "Depart, depart (O Father!), where our forefathers have already gone by the old paths (of the primitive Rishis). See there both the kings, Yama and the Divine Varuna, enjoying their immortal repast. Unite then in the highest heaven with Yama and the Fathers, having your good works following you. Giving up your vile (body) get to your abode and be again united with a body of great splendor!" So that the overthrow of death was complete.

Without going further with quotations and citations which, from their monotonous character, have, we fear, already become tedious, we may

---

[1] "Rig-veda," x. 121, 2.

now undertake to declare that the first of the two propositions, with which we commenced this discourse is proved, *viz.:*

" That the fundamental principles of Christian doctrine, in relation to the salvation of the world, find a remarkable counterpart in the Vedic principles of primitive Hinduism in relation to the destruction of sin and the redemption of the sinner by the efficacy of Sacrifice, itself a figure of *Prajâpati,* the Lord of the Creation, who had offered himself a sacrifice for that purpose."

All that has just been shown appertaining to the self-sacrifice of *Prajâpati* curiously resembles the Biblical description of CHRIST as God and man, our very Emmanuel, mortal and immortal, who "hath given Himself for us, an offering and a sacrifice to God for a sweet-smelling savor," of whom all previous sacrifices were but figures and reflections, who by His sacrifice or death hath "vanquished death, and brought life and immortality to light through the Gospel."

The Vedic ideal of *Prajâpati*, as we have seen, singularly approximates to the above description of our Lord, and therefore remarkably confirms the saving mysteries of Christianity.

We proceed now to discuss the second proposition: "That the meaning of *Prajâpati*—an appellation variously described as a *Purusha* begotten in the beginning, as *Visvakarman* the Creator of all—coincides with the meaning of the name and office of the historical reality JESUS CHRIST, and that no other person than JESUS of Nazareth has ever appeared in the world claiming the character and position of the self-sacrificing *Prajâpati*, half mortal and half immortal."

The name *Prajâpati* not only means "the Lord of Creatures," but also "the supporter, feeder, and deliverer of his creatures." The

(4)

great Vedic commentator Sàyaua interprets it in that wider sense. The Lord and Master has to feed and maintain his servants and subjects. The name, JESUS, in the Hebrew means the same. The radical term stands for *help*, *deliverance*, *salvation*. And that name was given Him because He would *save* His people from their sins. In the prophecy cited by Dr. Matthew, He is described as ἡγούμενος a leader or ruler, who "shall feed (ποιμανεῖ) my people Israel." He is therefore to His people what a shepherd is to his flock—both leader, ruler, and feeder. The same is the import of *pati ;* the name *Prajâpati*, therefore, singularly corresponds to the name JESUS.

Now in order to clear our way to the proper appreciation of this second proposition, it is necessary to consider that the doctrine of Sacrifice, as a figure of *Prajâpati* (who had offered himself as a sacrifice for the benefit of the world), did not long continue in its integrity among our forefathers ; but had fallen into oblivion even before the age of Buddha. The practice of sacrifice continued, indeed, but its origin and object, its chief characteristic as the good vessel which carries us over the waves of sin, as a figure or type of a self-sacrificing Saviour, had long vanished from the conceptions of our countrymen; so much so, that to some of us, both Hindus and Christians, it sounds, on first hearing it, as strange in our ears as the Gospel when first preached must have sounded in the ears of the people of Athens. But the *litera scripta* of the Vedas, in the providence of God, still remains, and tells us that the practice of Sacrifice, however lifeless, and therefore irksome it might have appeared in the age of Buddha, had nevertheless the stamp of universal truth at its commencement. We must, therefore, inquire what has become of that precious Truth ; what was the personality of *Prajâpati*, half mortal and half immortal, and how, and by what means, at the present time, we are to respond to the invitation of the "Rig-veda"; and embark on the good vessel which will carry us in safety over the waves of sin? What has become of those doctrines and practices now? We shall first consider the personality of *Prajâpati*. The appellative has been applied in the Hindu Scriptures to several characters. But one of these corresponds to the ideal of a *self-sacrificing Saviour of the world*.

Not a single character in the Hindu Pantheon, or in the Pantheon of any other nation, has claimed the position of one who offered himself as a sacrifice for the benefit of humanity. There is only one historical person, JESUS of Nazareth, whose name and position correspond to that of the Vedic ideal—one mortal and immortal, who sacrificed himself for mankind. By the process of exhaustion we may conclude that JESUS is the

true *Prajâpati*, the true Saviour of the world,
"the only Name given among men whereby we
must be saved." No other character, no other
historical personage can satisfy the lineaments
of the Vedic ideal. None else has even come
forward to claim that identity.

We are now in a position to say that the
precious truth we have been investigating,
though lost in India, is not lost to the world.
It was in fact a fragment of a great scheme of
salvation, which was at first partially revealed
and has since appeared in its integrity in the
Person of JESUS CHRIST—the true *Prajâpati* of
the world, and in His Church—the true Ark of
salvation, by which we may escape from the
waves of this sinful world. Do you wish to join
in the prayer to Varuna, the most ancient personality of God in the "Rig-veda": "O illustrious
Varuna, do thou quicken our understanding, we
that are practicing this ceremony, that we may

embark in the good ferrying boat by which we
may escape all sins?" Do you wish to embark
on that good navigating vessel? Hear the Vedas
then : "Sacrifice is the good ferrying boat"—
Sacrifice, the image of *Prajâpati* the self-sacrificing Deliverer of the world. And if *Prajâpati*
be found only in the Person of the historical
CHRIST, it will follow that the good navigating
vessel or Ark is no other than the Church of
CHRIST.

We think we may, therefore, declare our second
proposition to be also demonstrated. CHRIST is
the true *Prajâpati*—the true *Purusha* begotten
in the beginning before all worlds, and Himself
both God and man. The doctrines of saving
sacrifice the "primary religious rites" of the
"Rig-veda"—of the double character priest and
victim, variously called *Prajâpati*, *Purusha*,
and *Visvakarman*—of the Ark by which we
escape the waves of this sinful world—these doc-

trines, we say, which had appeared in our Vedas amid much rubbish, and things worse than rubbish, may be viewed as fragments of diamonds sparkling amid dust and mud, testifying to some invisible fabric of which they were component parts, and bearing witness like planets over a dark horizon to the absent sun of whom their refulgence was but a feeble reflection.

The gold has become dim by the alloy which has been mixed up by unholy and impure hands. As far, however, as the original Vedas refer to the self-devotion of "the Lord of Creatures," "begotten in the beginning," and to the primeval institution of sacrificial ceremonies as a typical "reflection" thereof, in which the sacrificer was himself the victim, they may be held, apart from subsequent concretions, to be evidences of ideas, originally pure, but afterwards debased under the corrupt suggestions of a wild imagination, in the absence of corrective influences. There are words and phrases among the citations made which cannot be accounted for, except as indications of something which underlay all sacrifices, such as those which Noah and Job had acceptably offered—something which related to Him *who gave His life a ransom for many*, and who was Himself the victim and Himself the priest. And so far the original legends of the Indo-Aryans are in their pristine purity strongly confirmatory of a fundamental principle of Christian doctrine.

All this may seem a strange saying to some, and a hard saying to others. But to the Hindu who reveres his Vedas, and the Christian who loves his Bible, to all who are friends of truth, it cannot be an unwelcome saying. Neither the Christian nor the Hindu, nor any sincere lover of truth can repine at this view of the fundamental teaching of the Vedas, calculated to bridge over the gulf which now separates relig-

ious minds of the West and the East. The
Vedas foreshow the Epiphany of CHRIST. The
Vedas shed a peculiar light upon that dispensa-
tion of Providence which brought Eastern sages
to worship CHRIST long before the Westerns have
even heard of Him.

The Christian, with the wide sympathy which
incites him to invite all nations to the faith of
CHRIST can only rejoice that the JESUS of the
Gospels respond to the self-sacrificing *Prajâpati*
of the Vedas, and that the evangelist's chief
work will be to exhibit, before his neighbors, the
true Ark of salvation—that true " vessel of sacrifice by which we may escape all sins." He will
only have to exhibit the real personality of the
true *Purusha* " begotten before the worlds,"
mortal and yet divine, " whose shadow, whose
death is immortality itself."

The tolerant Hindu, on the other hand, cannot
find any difficulty, any national humiliation, in

acknowledging the historical JESUS of the New Testament to correspond to the ideal *Prajâpati* of the Vedas, and to strengthen the corner-stone of the Vedic system, however corrupted by the impure accretions of ages, and disfigured by the rubbish of ignorance and caste-craft.

It is remarkable that while the elementary articles are so much alike, there is no rival hierarchy in India to declare for the ideal of the Vedic *Prajâpati*. The doctrine of a self-sacrificing Saviour, who by death overcame Death, appears to have vanished from the Sâstras without a representative succession. Although we have millions of gods in the Hindu Pantheon, yet we have none who proposes to be a substitute or successor of Him who offered Himself a sacrifice for the emancipation of mortals, and left the institution of Sacrifice as a "figure" of Himself. That doctrine has long become obsolete. The position of *Prajâpati*, himself the

priest and himself the victim, no member of that
Pantheon has dared to occupy. His throne is
vacant, and his crown without an owner. No
one now can claim that crown and that throne in
the hearts of Hindus, who are true to the original teaching of the Vedas, so rightfully as the
historical JESUS, who in name and character, as
we have seen, closely resembles our primitive
Prajâpati. We have known good Christian
people stand aghast at all these ideas. We
do not wonder at it. Even in apostolic times,
Peter was impeached for consorting with "men
uncircumcised," and much evidence had to be
adduced before the brethren could hold their
peace and glorify God, saying, "Then hath God
also to the Gentiles granted repentance unto
life." So long have Hindus been classed with
inveterate idolators and Gentiles, that some may
well be amazed at finding germs of Christian
mysteries in the heathen Vedas. But facts can-

not be denied, we cannot shut our eyes to actual
realities.   Instead of indulging in mere feelings
of wonder, let us give glory to God, whose mercy
and grace cannot be contracted within the nar-
row limits of our puny ideas.   Nor is there any
reason here for doing otherwise than extolling
God for having vouchsafed so much light, more
perhaps than we could have expected *a priori*,
to certain Indian Rishis.   We must remember
that the distinguished man, so much honored
in the Bible, who bore the title of "King of
Righteousness," to whom Abraham himself
gave tithes, and who was an acknowledged type
of CHRIST, was himself a Gentile.

The Veda tells us of the Ark of Salvation by
which sin may be escaped, and repeatedly ex-
horts us to embark in it.   The Ark of Salvation,
with the *Purusha* begotten in the beginning
at its head, can be no other than the Church of
Christ.   In addition, then, to the exhortations of

Christian evangelists, we have our own Vedas calling on us to embark on that very Ark, if we desire to be delivered from the waves of sin. The doctrine which had become obsolete and fallen into oblivion by lurking in the sealed manuscripts of the Vedas, has been, in the Providence of God, restored. It appears now as an abiding witness for the Christian faith. An eloquent preacher once remarked with reference to the Vedic doctrines already alluded to here, that no person can be a true Hindu without being a true Christian. The relation between Vedic doctrines and Christianity is indeed so intimate that we can scarcely hold the one without being led to the other, much less can we keep our hold on the one while resisting the claims of the other.